Reggie

KID PENGUIN

ABOUT THIS BOOK

This book was edited by Esther Cajahuaringa, art directed by David Caplan, and designed by Prashansa Thapa. The production was supervised by Bernadette Flinn, and the production editor was Marisa Finkelstein. The text was set in the creator's hand-lettered font, and the display type was hand-lettered by the creator.

This book is a work of fiction. Names, characters, places, and incidents are the product of the author's imagination or are used fictitiously. Any resemblance to actual events, locales, or persons, living or dead, is coincidental. · Copyright © 2023 by Jennifer de Oliveira · Cover illustration copyright © 2023 by Jennifer de Oliveira · Cover design by Prashansa Thapa · Cover copyright © 2023 by Hachette Book Group, Inc. · Hachette Book Group supports the right to free expression and the value of copyright. The purpose of copyright is to encourage writers and artists to produce the creative works that enrich our culture. · The scanning, uploading, and distribution of this book without permission is a theft of the author's intellectual property. If you would like permission to use material from the book (other than for review purposes), please contact permissions@hbgusa.com. Thank you for your support of the author's rights. · Little, Brown Ink · Hachette Book Group · 1290 Avenue of the Americas, New York, NY 10104 · Visit us at LBYR.com · First Edition: June 2023 · Little, Brown Ink is an imprint of Little, Brown and Company. The Little, Brown Ink name and logo are trademarks of Hachette Book Group, Inc. · The publisher is not responsible for websites (or their content) that are not owned by the publisher. · Little, Brown and Company books may be purchased in bulk for business, educational, or promotional use. For information, please contact your local bookseller or the Hachette Book Group Special Markets Department at special.markets@hbgusa.com. · Library of Congress Cataloging-in-Publication Data · Names: Oliveira, Jen de, author, illustrator. · Title: Reggie: kid penguin / Jen de Oliveira. · Description: First edition. | New York : Little, Brown and Company, 2023. | Series: Reggie ; 1 | Audience: Ages 4–8. | Summary: "Reginald 'Reggie' Guinn is a kid penguin who is equal parts playful, curious, and cantankerous, and gets into everyday adventures at school, home, and his neighborhood." —Provided by publisher. · Identifiers: LCCN 2021051008 | ISBN 9780759557550 (hardcover) | ISBN 9780759557567 (trade paperback) | ISBN 9780759557543 (ebook) · Subjects: CYAC: Graphic novels. | Penguins—Fiction. | LCGFT: Graphic novels. · Classification: LCC PZ7.7.O427 Re 2023 | DDC 741.5/973—dc23/eng/20220201 · LC record available at https://lccn.loc.gov/2021051008 · ISBNs: 978-0-7595-5755-0 (hardcover), 978-0-7595-5756-7 (pbk.), 978-0-7595-5754-3 (ebook), 978-0-316-38422-3 (ebook), 978-0-316-38427-8 (ebook) · PRINTED IN CHINA · APS · Hardcover: 10 9 8 7 6 5 4 3 2 1 · Paperback: 10 9 8 7 6 5 4 3 2 1

FOR MY MAMA, VICKEY

Reggie

KID PENGUIN

THAT'S ME!

JEN de OLIVEIRA

LB
INK

LITTLE, BROWN AND COMPANY
NEW YORK · BOSTON

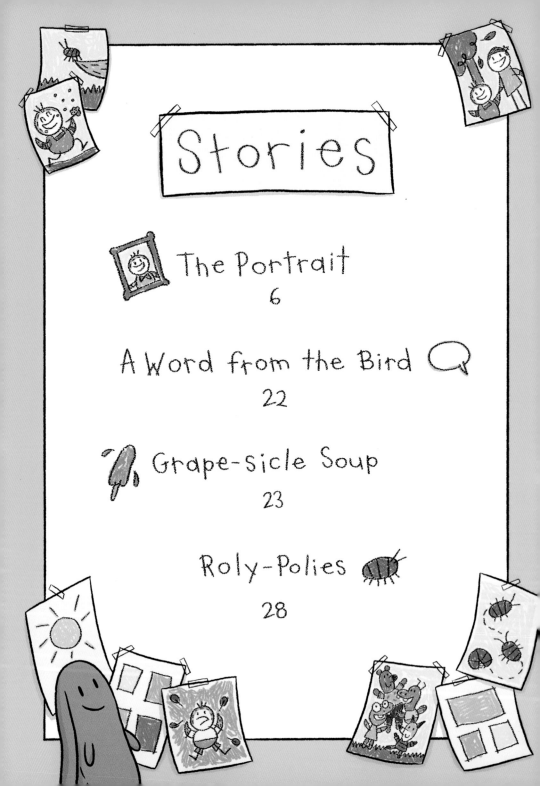

Stories

MY FAVORITE STORY IS...
<u>ALL</u> OF THEM!

The Portrait

THE LIGHTS ARE WAY TOO BRIGHT!

MY EYES!

THE PICTURE TAKERS YELL AT ME!

SIT UP STRAIGHT!

SMILE!

OVER HERE!

LOOK UP!

A REAL SMILE!

THEY TWIST MY BODY IN WEIRD WAYS!

TILT YOUR HEAD A BIT MORE.

POINT YOUR FEET THIS WAY!

FLIPPERS TOGETHER!

AND MY PICTURES ALWAYS TURN OUT BAD!

SAY CHEESE!

ACHOoo!

CLICK!

REGGIE, DON'T COMPLAIN.

NOW TAKE THIS SWEATER TO YOUR ROOM AND GET DRESSED.

BUT--

THAT ONE HAS AN ITCHY TAG!

SIGH

TAP!
TAP!
TAP!

SQUEEZE...

SPLORT!

GRAB!

WIPE!

WIPE!

UH-OH...

IT'S STUCK!

LATER.

I THINK IT TURNED OUT PRETTY GOOD!

WHAT DO YOU THINK, MAMA?

WELL...

IT ACTUALLY MAY BE YOUR BEST PORTRAIT YET!

YEAH!

Grape-sicle Soup

=DING!=

=DING!=

ONE GRAPE-SICLE, PLEASE!

GREAT.

THE NEXT DAY.

ONE GRAPE-SICLE, PLEASE!

TIP!

TIP!

TRAS

NICE WORK, REGGIE!

MAYBE THE ROLY-POLIES ARE HUNGRY.

HAROLD, GET MORE PLANTS FOR THE RESTAURANT.

OKAY!

NOW SERVING THE MAYOR'S SPECIAL!

THEY'RE ACTUALLY DANDELIONS.

YOU KNOW...

I'LL BET THE ROLY-POLIES WOULD LIKE THEIR OWN PLAYGROUND!

I'LL BRING THE TIRE SWING!

I'VE GOT THE SLIDE!

DON'T FORGET THE MAYOR'S OFFICE!

I THINK THEY LIKE IT!

HEY, LOOK!

MR. O!

LEGGY'S USING THE TIRE SWING!

43

GRAB! GRAB!

I'M MAKING A COMIC.

YOU WANT TO SEE IT?

OKAY. YOU CAN READ IT WHILE I GET A SNACK.

Cookie Dough
A comic by
Reggie

One day, Mama was making chocolate chip cookies.

choco chips

When she wasn't looking, I ate a spoonful of cookie dough.

CHOMP!

Okay. Four spoonfuls.

CHOMP!

CHOMP!

CHOMP!

CHOMP!

Then I went outside to play. It was sunny and very hot.

I'm pretty sure the hot, hot sun started baking the cookies--right in my tummy!

Oh no!

SIZZLE! SIZZLE!

48

I could feel the cookies getting BIGGER.

My tummy started to hurt.

UGGGGHHHHHHHH!

GURGLE!

GURGLE!

RUMBLE!

RUMBLE!

It hurt _so_ much, I didn't even want the cookies Mama brought out for me.

NOOOO!!!

GURGLE!

GRUMBLE!

After that, I learned my lesson...

I only eat cookie dough on very cold days.

CHOMP!

That way, the cookies won't bake inside me.

Kid Leash

NOT THE LEASH!

RUN!

GRAB!

STRUGGLE!

REGGIE!

WHAT ARE YOU DOING?

HUFF!
HUFF!

WHOA!

THANK YOU SO MUCH!

HIS NAME IS REGGIE.

REGGIE, YOU WERE VERY BRAVE AND SELFLESS!

YOU MUST BE SO PROUD.

BYE, DOGGY!

-PANT- -PANT-

-PANT- -PANT-

GRRRR!

Bedtime

FINE!

SOON.

AHH...

FWIP!

FLOOF!

GOOD NIGHT, BUBBA.

PAT
PAT

NIGHT-NIGHT, ROONEY.